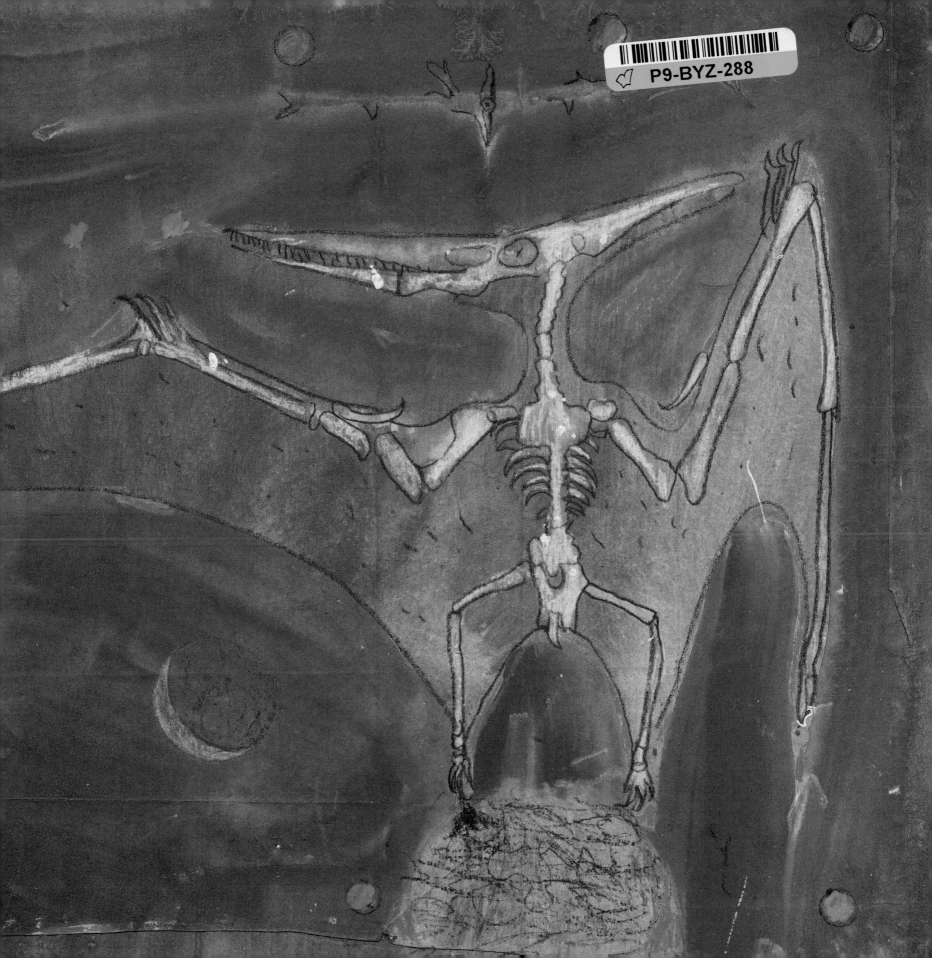

DINOTHESAURUS

prehistoric poems and paintings by douglas florian

beach lane books   new york   london   toronto   sydney

50°

40°

30°

20°

10°

*In memory of **Alegria Fallouz**,*
a kind, sweet soul who passed away too soon,
and now resides in heaven

CONTENTS

There once was a spinste
Endowed with such delic
That she thought

The Age of Dinosaurs

The dinosaurs
First lived outdoors
During the time *Triassic*.
While most died out,
Some came about
Later in the *Jurassic*.
Then they evolved,
As Earth revolved,
In times known as *Cretaceous*.
But now indoors
Great dinosaurs
Fill museum halls, *spacious*.

Brachiosaurus

BRAK-ee-oh-SAW-rus (arm lizard)

Longer than a tennis court.
Bigger than a barge.
I never knew a lizard
Could ever be so large.
It moved about within a herd
That roamed across a plain.
With stretched-out neck, high as a bird,
It looked much like a crane.
On massive legs with knobby knees,
It traveled very s l o w
And ate all day from tops of trees—
Grow, baby, grow!

CRANE

Stegosaurus

steg-oh-SAW-rus (roof lizard)

Ste-go-SAUR-us
Her-bi-VOR-ous
Dined on plants inside the forest.
Bony plates grew on its back,
Perhaps to guard it from attack.
Or to help identify
A Stegosaurus girl or guy.
Its brain was smaller than a plum.
Stegosaurus was quite DUMB.

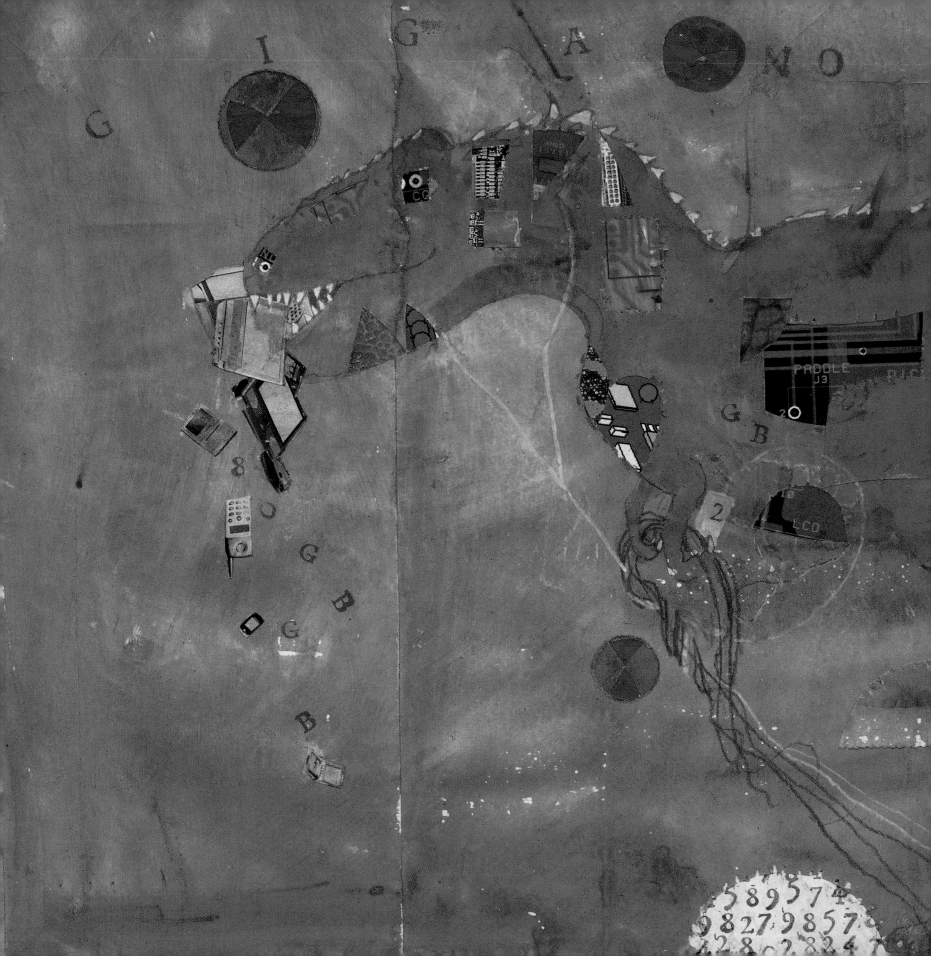

Giganotosaurus

JIG-ah-not-oh-SAW-rus (giant southern lizard)

One hundred million years before us
Lived the Giga-not-o-saurus.
Gigantic, titanic, enormous, colossal—
What once was humongous is now just a fossil.
When it was hungry or got into fights,
It opened its jaws and took **giga-bites**.

Plesiosaurs

PLEASE-ee-oh-sawrs (near lizards)

We're PLEASE-ee-oh-sawrs. We're car-ni-vores.
We swim in deep seas, unlike dinosaurs.
We swallow sea reptiles and gobble great fishes.
A fine meal of mollusk tastes jolly delicious.
But we aren't vicious, we're very polite—
We always say PLEASE before we might bite.

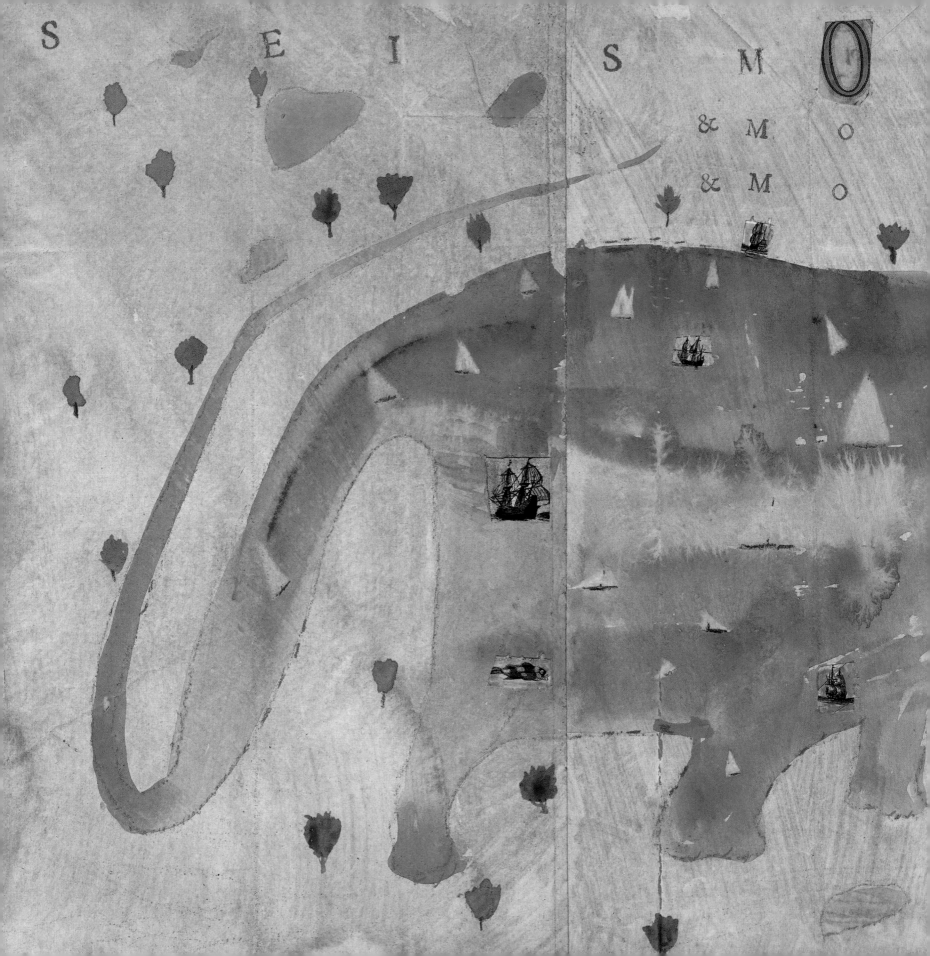

SIZE WISE

Seismosaurus

SIZE-mo-SAW-rus (earthshaking lizard)

Seismosaurus: tremendous in size.
Seismosaurus: stupendous lengthwise.
Seismosaurus: could make the earth shake.
Seismosaurus: as large as a lake.

Baryonyx

BARE-ee-ON-icks (heavy claw)

He had a huge and heavy claw
    And crocodile-like skull.
A lashing, slashing dino-saw—
    A sharpie, never dull.
His claws and jaws and pointed teeth
    Were fashioned to attack.
If Bary you should ever meet—
    Ask him to scratch your back.

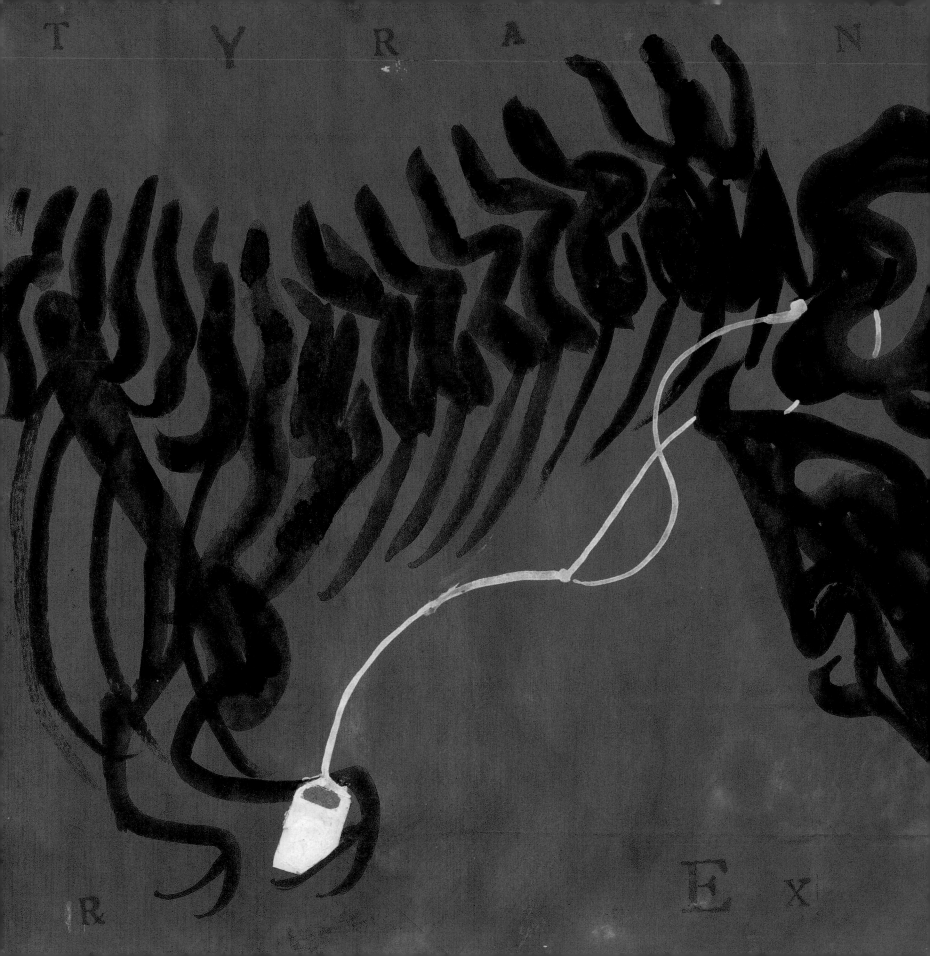

TYRANN

R   E x

NOSAURUS

Tyrannosaurus rex

ty-ran-oh-SAW-rus REX (king of tyrant lizards)

Some forty feet long.
Some fourteen feet tall.
Its back limbs were strong.
Its front limbs were small.
Its eyesight was keen.
Its hunger voracious.
This creature was seen
In times called Cretaceous.
Its jaws were horrific.
Its profile distinct.
I find it terrific
That it's T-rex-tinct.

Iguanodon

ih-GWAH-no-don (iguana tooth)

I wouldn't wanna come upon
The ten-foot-tall Iguanodon.
But if one day Iguanodon
I came upon, I'd wanna
Ask that big IguanoDON:
Where is IguanoDONNA?

Triceratops

try-SAIR-a-tops (three-horned face)

Triceratops.
Try-scare-a-tops.
Try-wouldn't-want-to-dare-a-tops.
Triceratops.
Try-stare-a-tops.
Beware-and-please-take-care-a-tops.
Born with three great horns in place,
Triceratops was **in your face.**

ri·cer·a·tops (tri
dinosaurs of the ge
ceous Period, havir
horn over each ey
1890–95; < NL < G
ERAT-), + ops face

any of various
of the late Creta-
n the neck, a long
horn on the nose.
ee-horned (see TRI

SAURUS

Ankylosaurus
AN-kee-lo-SAW-rus (fused lizard)

Tough as tanks and hard as nails.
Heavy clubs swing from our tails.
We like spikes and we like scutes
(Bony plates we wear as suits).
We have heavy-armored skin—
Hey, but that's the skin we're in!

Barosaurus

BAR-oh-SAW-rus (heavy lizard)

I'm higher than five elephants.
I'm longer than most whales.
My giant neck is balanced by
My forty-three-foot tail.
A tail that is my weapon.
It swings from side to side.
From nose to tail I'm ninety feet—
Hey kid, ya wanna ride?

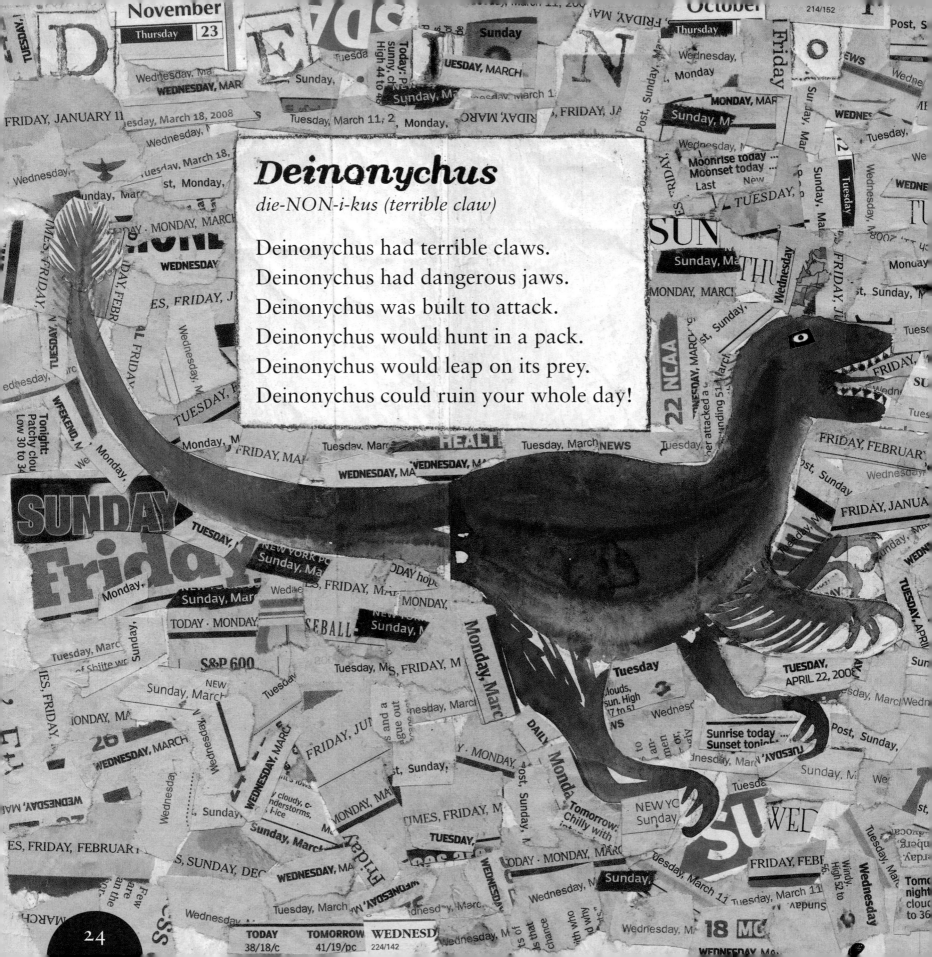

Deinonychus

die-NON-i-kus (terrible claw)

Deinonychus had terrible claws.
Deinonychus had dangerous jaws.
Deinonychus was built to attack.
Deinonychus would hunt in a pack.
Deinonychus would leap on its prey.
Deinonychus could ruin your whole day!

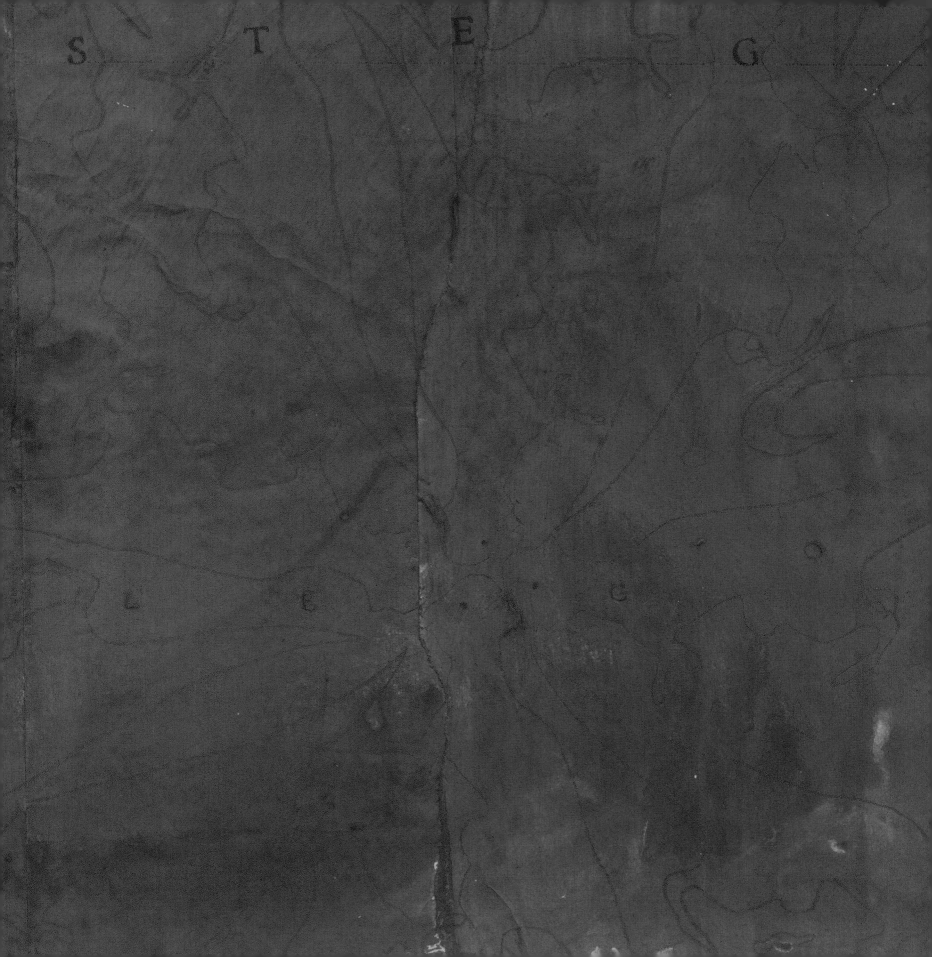

Stegoceras

steg-OSS-er-us (roof horn)

Thick head. Brick head. Hard head, too.
Round head. Mound head. Odd head, you.
Bone head. Stone head. Head like a dome.
Bash head. Smash head. Then *head* home.

Micropachycephalosaurus

mike-row-pack-ee-SEF-a-low-SAW-rus (small, thickheaded lizard)

20
Inches
Long—you're small.
Don't seem a dinosaur at all.
You have a frail and fragile frame.
And how do you pronounce your name?

TROH-oh-don (wounding tooth)

Said to be brainy.
Said to be bright.
But what did it read?
And what did it write?
Said to be crafty.
Said to be smart.
But did it make music?
Or did it do art?
Said to be witty
And wise when it thinked.
If it was so smart,
How come it's extinct?

P T E R O

Pterosaurs

TERR-oh-sawrs (winged lizards)

The pterrifying pterosaurs
Flew ptours the ptime of dinosaurs.
With widespread wings and pteeth pto ptear,
They pterrorized the pteeming air.
They were not ptame.
They were ptenacious—
From the Ptriassic
Pto the Cretaceous.

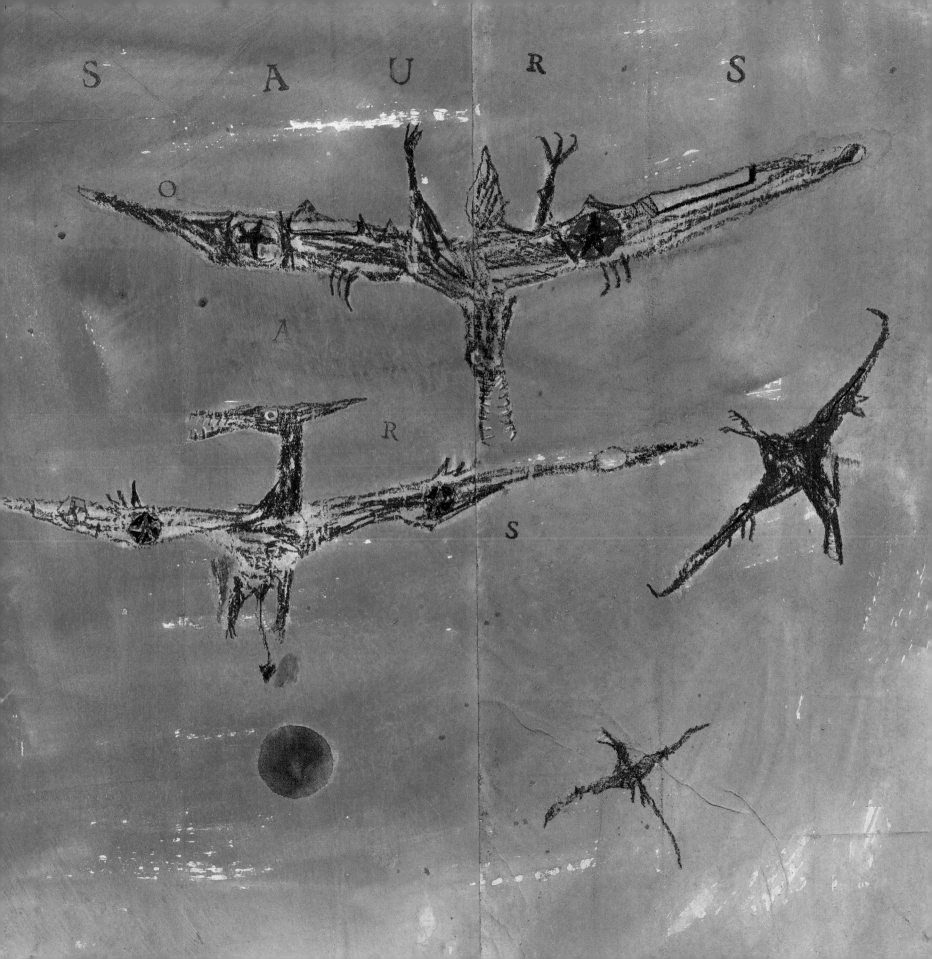

Minmi

MIN-me (named after the Minmi Crossing in Australia)

What's Minmi's BIGGEST claim to fame?
It has the smallest dinosaur name.

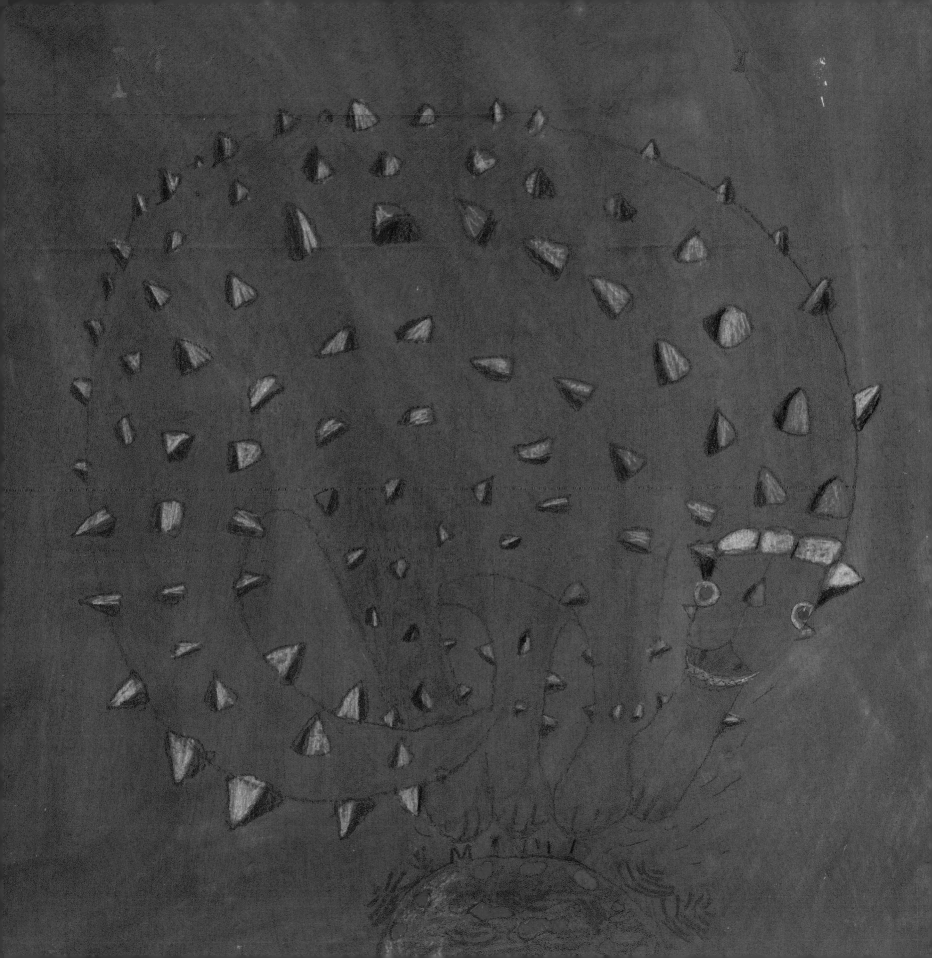

Spinosaurus

SPY-no-SAW-rus (spine lizard)

What kept the Spinosaurus warm
When it was colder than the norm?

Spines much like a solar panel.
(And long underwear of flannel.)

What made the dinosaurs die out?
Why don't they still parade about?
Maybe volcanic ash and smoke
Filled the air and made them ch-ch-choke.
Or else a crashing meteorite
Exploded, blocking all the light.
As weather changes ran amok,
The dinosaurs ran out of luck.
The climate on the Earth grew c-c-cold,
And many plants died out, I'm told,
Which killed most of the herbivores
And consequently carnivores.
What made the dinosaurs extinct?
What do **you** say? What do **you** think?
Next time you go to a museum,
Ask some dinosaurs—if you see 'em!

GLOSSARYSAURUS

The Age of Dinosaurs

The age of dinosaurs was during the Mesozoic era of life on Earth. This era is broken into three periods: the Triassic, the Jurassic, and the Cretaceous. The dinosaurs first appeared about 235 million years ago, during the Triassic, a period of time from 251 to 200 million years ago. Crocodiles, turtles, frogs, and small mammals also evolved during this time. The Jurassic period, from 200 to 145 million years ago, saw the emergence of the huge plant eaters, such as *Brachiosaurus* and *Barosaurus*, as well as the large predators, such as *Allosaurus*. The final period of dinosaurs, the Cretaceous, lasted from 145 to 65 million years ago. During this time a vast array of dinosaurs evolved, such as the predatory *Tyrannosaurus rex*, the intelligent troodonts, and the armored ankylosaurs.

Brachiosaurus

About eighty-five feet long and taller than a three-story building, *Brachiosaurus* was one of the largest dinosaurs. Its stretched-out neck supported a small head with large nostrils. Many scientists think its long front legs helped it feed on leaves from the tops of trees, much as giraffes do today.

Stegosaurus

Stegosaurus had large bony plates running along its back. It may have used these plates as protection from attack, or to help identify a male or female member of its species. *Stegosaurus* had a very small brain compared to its body size, making it one of the least-intelligent dinosaurs.

Giganotosaurus

This gigantic beast was one of the biggest meat-eating dinosaurs. Its head had large eyes and massive jaws filled with serrated teeth. The bones of *Giganotosaurus* were first discovered in Argentina, where it lived in warm swamps and preyed on huge plant-eating dinosaurs such as *Argentinosaurus*.

Plesiosaurs

Plesiosaurs were prehistoric reptiles of the sea, but not true dinosaurs, as dinosaurs were terrestrial (lived on land). They had four winglike flippers to help them swim through water. Unlike fish, they came up to the surface to breathe air. Some had large heads and short necks, while others had small heads and very long necks. All died out at the same time as the dinosaurs.

Seismosaurus

Seismosaurus may have been the longest dinosaur that ever lived. Some scientists believe it to be a variation of another dinosaur, *Diplodocus*. The only known *Seismosaurus* skeleton was discovered in 1979 in New Mexico. Because of its incredible size, it took thirteen years to excavate.

Baryonyx

Baryonyx, meaning "heavy claw," had a twelve-inch curved claw on each hand. It used these claws, along with its crocodile-like jaws, to catch fish along riverbanks. The nickname of *Baryonyx* is Claws.

Tyrannosaurus rex

Also known as *T. rex*, this dinosaur was one of the most ferocious carnivores that ever lived. It is also the most famous, having been featured in many movies. Scientists disagree whether *Tyrannosaurus rex* ran fast or slow and whether it was a predator, a scavenger, or both.

Iguanodon

Iguanodon probably walked on all four legs but reared up on its hind legs to eat leaves from trees. Its thumb spikes were used for defense and perhaps to break open fruit for food.

Triceratops

The strong, solid skull of *Triceratops* had two large brow horns and one short nose horn. These were probably used in combat with its rivals. The large bony frill at the back of its head protected its neck and made its head appear larger.

Ankylosaurus

The thick, tough skin of this herbivore was covered with bony plates and rows of spikes as a defense against predators. It also used its large clubbed tail for protection. This massive creature weighed about five tons and grew to thirty-five feet in length.

Barosaurus

This dinosaur had a very long neck and tail, but short legs and a tiny head. Its tail ended in a whiplash, which it used for defense. It fed on plants throughout the plains of North America. The rearing *Barosaurus* skeleton exhibited at the American Museum of Natural History is the tallest mounted skeleton in the world.

Deinonychus

This predator used its sharp curved claws and powerful jaws to kill its prey. It was built for speed and probably hunted in packs. *Deinonychus* was about ten feet long and weighed about 180 pounds. It was likely warm-blooded and had feathers.

Stegoceras

Stegoceras had a three-inch-thick dome of solid bone at the top of its skull. This was likely used as a battering ram against its rivals. Its small sawlike teeth were good for feeding on leaves and fruit.

Micropachycephalosaurus

Despite being one of the smallest dinosaurs, *Micropachycephalosaurus* has the longest dinosaur name, with twenty-three letters. This herbivore was only about fifteen inches tall and twenty inches long.

Troodon

This small dinosaur had a large brain compared to its body size and is therefore thought to have been intelligent. It was named *Troodon* ("wounding tooth") after its small, sharp teeth. Its large eyes indicate that it probably hunted at night. It may have been warm-blooded and covered with feathers.

Pterosaurs

Pterosaurs were flying prehistoric reptiles, but not dinosaurs, as true dinosaurs were terrestrial. They flew on wings of skin that stretched from their bodies to the tips of their long wing-fingers. Their delicate bones were extremely light and their wingspans could reach more than thirty feet.

Minmi

Discovered in Australia, *Minmi* has the shortest dinosaur name, unless you include the Chinese dinosaur *Mei*, which is more commonly called *Mei long*. *Minmi* had an armored body and ate fruit and low-lying plants such as ferns.

Spinosaurus

Spinosaurus had a "sail" made of long spines and skin that rose as many as six feet from its back. This sail may have helped it absorb heat when it was cold, radiate heat when it was hot, and tell related species apart.

The End of Dinosaurs

Scientists are not sure what caused the mass extinction of the dinosaurs at the end of the Cretaceous period. Perhaps a large meteorite or comet struck the Earth, throwing up enough dust to block the sunlight for many years. This could have caused Earth's atmosphere to cool, killing plants, the herbivores that fed on those plants, as well as the carnivores that fed on the herbivores. Volcanoes, spewing up hot ash into the skies, may have also caused a massive climate change that brought about the end of dinosaurs. Although the prehistoric dinosaurs are long gone, their footprints, bones, and impressions continue to amaze us, and they live on in their modern-day descendants, the birds.

Dinosaur Museums and Fossil Sites

American Museum of Natural History
New York, New York, USA
www.amnh.org
Researchers from this museum have gone on many fossil field trips since 1897. One group of researchers discovered the first skeleton of *Tyrannosaurus rex* in 1902. The museum contains the largest collection of dinosaur fossils in the world. More than one hundred specimens are displayed in its two dinosaur halls.

Smithsonian Institution National Museum of Natural History
Washington, DC, USA
www.mnh.si.edu
More than 1,500 dinosaur specimens are housed in this museum. About thirty mounted skeletons are on display, including a spectacular *Triceratops*.

The Field Museum
Chicago, Illinois, USA
www.fieldmuseum.org
This museum contains dinosaur fossils from every major dinosaur group. It has Sue, the world's largest and most complete *Tyrannosaurus rex*, and *Cryolophosaurus*, one of the first dinosaurs found in Antarctica.

Royal Tyrrell Museum
Alberta, Canada
www.tyrrellmuseum.com
Located near Dinosaur Provincial Park, this museum exhibits hundreds of dinosaur fossils, as well as a life-size model of a prehistoric reef and a living Cretaceous garden with more than six hundred kinds of plants. Visitors can also watch scientists prepare fossils for research and exhibition.

Museum of the Rockies
Montana State University
Bozeman, Montana, USA
www.museumoftherockies.org
The Siebel Dinosaur Complex in this museum contains the largest *Tyrannosaurus rex* skull ever found, some of the rarest fossil samples in the world, and dinosaur embryos and nests.

Hell Creek Formation
Montana, USA
The Hell Creek area of Montana has produced many dinosaur fossils from the late Cretaceous period. Researcher Barnum Brown discovered the first skeleton of *Tyrannosaurus rex* here. Other dinosaur specimens found here include *Ankylosaurus*, *Troodon*, *Triceratops*, and *Pachycephalosaurus*.

Dinosaur National Monument
Utah, USA
www.nps.gov/dino
This site was discovered in 1909 by paleontologist Earl Douglass. The exposed wall of sandstone Douglass found here contains 1,500 fossil bones, including those of *Stegosaurus* and *Barosaurus*.

Selected Bibliography and Further Reading

Bingham, Caroline. *First Dinosaur Encyclopedia*. New York: DK Publishing, 2006.

Dixon, Dougal. *The Illustrated Encyclopedia of Dinosaurs*. London: Lorenz Books, 2006.

Holtz, Thomas R., Jr., and Luis V. Rey. *Dinosaurs: The Most Complete, Up-to-Date Encyclopedia for Dinosaur Lovers of All Ages*. New York: Random House Books for Young Readers, 2007.

Mash, Robert. *How to Keep Dinosaurs*. London: Orion, 2004.

With thanks to Mike Shoulders for his prescient suggestion of a title.

BEACH LANE BOOKS * An imprint of Simon & Schuster Children's Publishing Division * 1230 Avenue of the Americas, New York, New York 10020 * Copyright © 2009 by Douglas Florian * All rights reserved, including the right of reproduction in whole or in part in any form. BEACH LANE BOOKS is a trademark of Simon & Schuster, Inc. * For information about special discounts for bulk purchases, please contact Simon & Schuster Special Sales at 1-866-506-1949 or business@simonandschuster.com. * The Simon & Schuster Speakers Bureau can bring authors to your live event. For more information or to book an event, contact the Simon & Schuster Speakers Bureau at 1-866-248-3049 or visit our website at www.simonspeakers.com. * Book design by Ann Bobco and Michael McCartney * The text for this book is set in Sabon LT. * The illustrations for this book were done with gouache, collage, colored pencils, stencils, dinosaur dust, and rubber stamps on primed brown paper bags. * Manufactured in China * Library of Congress Cataloging-in-Publication Data * Florian, Douglas. * Dinothesaurus : prehistoric poems and paintings / by Douglas Florian. * p. cm. * ISBN 978-1-4169-7978-4 * 1. Dinosaurs—Juvenile poetry. 2. Children's poetry, American. I. Title. * PS3556.L589D56 2009 * 811'.54—dc22 * 2007045433 * 10 9 8 7 6 0913 SCP

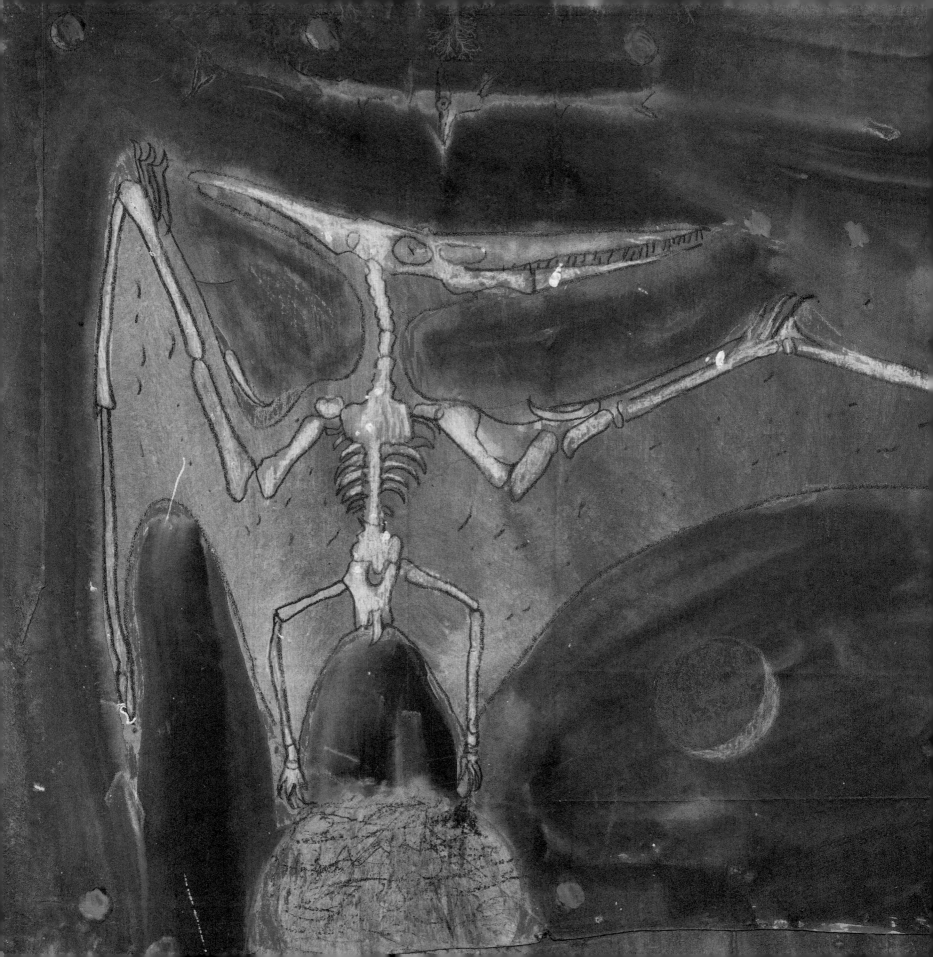